A LOBSTER TALE

Largo & Roe

A Lobster Tale, Largo & Roe

ISBN: 979-8-9925199-2-1 (e-book) ISBN: 979-8-9925199-1-4 (softback)

ISBN: 979-8-9925199-3-8 (hardcover) Library of Congress Control Number: 2025908446

Publisher's Cataloging-in-Publication Data

provided by Five Rainbows Cataloging Services

Names: Piccolo, J. Renee, author.

Title: A lobster tale : largo & roe / J. Renee Piccolo.

Description: Pompano Beach, FL : Publishing Chalet, 2025. | Summary: A story of nautical puns and idioms for everyone. | Audience: Grades 7 & up.Identifiers: LCCN 2025908446 (print) | ISBN 979-8-9925199-3-8 (hardcover) | ISBN 979-8-9925199-1-4 (paperback) | ISBN 979-8-9925199-2-1 (ebook)Subjects: LCSH: Young adult fiction. | Lobsters--Juvenile fiction. | CYAC: Lobsters--Fiction. | Ocean--Fiction. | Sea stories. | Fantasy fiction. | BISAC: YOUNG ADULT FICTION / Animals / Marine Life. | YOUNG ADULT FICTION / Fantasy / General. | YOUNG ADULT FICTION / Science & Nature / General. | YOUNG ADULT FICTION / Fantasy / Romance. Classification: LCC PZ7.1.P53 Lo 2025 (print) | LCC PZ7.1.P53 (ebook) | DDC [Fic]--dc23.

A LOBSTER TALE

Largo & Roe

Novella, By

J. RENEE PICCOLO

A Lobster Tale, Largo & Roe

Dedication

Have you wanted to escape reality, like a lobster in a hotpot? Put on your life vest for a rare blue lobster's quest to freedom, as he overcomes insecurities, battles anxieties, and adapts to environmental changes. Finding love and friendship through hardship. A story of nautical puns and idioms for everyone.

Written without chapters, traps nor limitations in four parts to honor the lobster's four-part body: head, limbs, stomach, tail. Which will you think with?

Table of Contents

Glossary

Roe – Resilient Red Lobster
Largo – Courageous, Rare Blue Lobster
Mama-Rouge – Roe's Talented Mother
Paparoa- Roe's Brave Father
Twin-Roe- Roe's Tough Sibling
Grandpa-Lob, Grandma-Lob – Roe's Wise Grandparents
Delphine – Quirky, Dependable Dolphin
Slate – Protective, Stubborn Shark
Magdeline- Creative, Collector Manatee
Octavia – Curious, Clever Octopus
Scuzzy and Scoozy – Misfit Sibling Squids
Captain Wry-fi- Villainous Restauranteur Sailor
Captain Laiz – Villainous Brother
Mrs. Wits and Mrs. Waverly– Captains' Wives
Giacomo – Heroic Student
Ms. Manners –Teacher
Lil' Roux – Azul and Amarillo –Yellow/Blue Lobster Offspring

Part One:

Life of Little Roe

On the Atlantic coast of Florida was a small lobster named Roe. Born without Floridian claws did not stop the bottom feeder from defending her family's rock oasis at two inches big. Tiny, spiny, and rather mighty than difficult to handle. She wondered about treasures buried on distant shores. The red lobster made more than a splash, a cannonball!

At the end of a long pier lived, Mama-Rouge and Paparoa, Grandparent-Lobs, and Twin-Roe. Together, constructing discreet homes in rocky crevices.

During the day, they like to rest. At night, Grandpa-Lob and Paparoa explored the ocean floor. The twins stayed home, spritzing salty water with lemon peels from overboard meals for sun-kissed shells.

Youthful spirits, full of exhilaration.

Endless nights of sea moss pillow-talking. Balancing seaworms on their heads while rocking on Grandma-Lob's abandoned chair after school, unable to forget fish odors of her shaggy, fungoid carpeting. The tacky seawall paper was atrocious.

Best friends chasing fish tails- making priceless memories.

The world is their oyster, and they knew it.

The half-moon shined from afar. Paparoa caught herring appetizers to feast on, while listening for intruders- way too close for comfort. Grandma-Lob's in the galley way cooking delicious southern scampi with algae grits and sea salt.

"Moderation is key, never bite off more than you can chew," said Mama-Rouge, staying on track with favored plant-based diets and strict cardio regimes. Suddenly, Twin-Roe shouted, "A boat is coming our way! Curl your tail. We should get inside!"

The sisters eager to learn more after being alarmed, "How did Grandpa-Lob build a home on the pier? How is he almost one hundred years old?" Too many questions, they ponder.

Thunder rumbled with intervals of lightning. Grandpa-Lob stayed in for the night, he lives two rocks down.

"OG-lob, so happy to see you! Please tell us more about the boats, sister and I noticed lights flashing while you were out exploring last night."

In a raspy wise voice, with accumulated stacked gold chains and salty eyes, he replied, "That's the lobstermen, who likes to visit the pier with a bucket of bait, taking us to our impending doom. You're too smart to be trapped."

Describing in more detail, "Many moons ago, I ventured out to the reef hungry for snails. A net fell on me, Lobstermen put me in their boat headed to shore. After measuring me over five inches and offering a fish treat, he threw me back to sea. Made my way home to Grandma-Lob with the earth's magnetic superpowers. Before we met, I somehow lived in a supermarket aquarium for ten lonely years, until released out of pity. You're still too young to leave the pier. For now, stay close and trade silkworms with your squat lobster cousin."

"Thanks Grandpa, you have the best tales! We hope to meet someone brave as you someday!"

"If you believe, the stars will always align a beautiful life for you. Dreams are good to have; they take you places you can only dream," he said, "best we turn on our heads for bed, night-night termite."

That morning, Mama-Rouge alerts the twins that sea friends will be over to celebrate their birthdays, "No littering water balloons at this party. Instead, dissolvable sassy-string! It's Sunday fun' day, all day until Monday!" she told them.

That year, they grew three inches bigger - careful of the scarcity stick. The tweens are ready for their first big outing.

Tap, tap, tap...

"Are we there yet, Paparoa?"

"Almost, another mile to go!"

Gaining momentum, a frightening dark shadow approached, "Hey, what's eaten ya!?" asked a big-headed fish, in a British accent.

"Ha-ha, not funny," said Paparoa, "we're on a journey to the coral lagoon."

"Calm down its me, Slate, no reason to go off the deep end. I'll be your chaperon!"

"Thanks, you can be bull-headed at times," Paparoa jokes, "Slate is a bull shark."

"Hey, who's laughing at me? Your dad and I've been friends forty years!"

"That's right! Slate, our hometown hero keeping a watchful eye showed up one night as two men wrapped fishing line around me. Wrestling in panic, Mama-Rouge and Grandma-Lob were taken aback, terrified. Slate bumped the Captain's boat, causing them to zoom off disappointment. Ever since, we've been close chums - incredible friends."

Startled by colorful living anemone, they had arrived at the lagoon. Slate needed to rest, "Now that's worth fishing for..." he mumbled, dozing off at the beauty.

The lobster family continued to explore, "Wow, sea glass! Mama-Rouge can add it to her shell necklaces," said Roe.

"So thoughtful. Grandma-Lob always complains the water is too warm. Would she like this sea fan?" asked twin, "all we need is a souvenir for Grandpa-Lob."

"Good mawnin!" said Magdaline the manatee, in her native Bahamian accent. "A beautiful day! I slept super-duper. Did a little bit of sand exfoliating on my blubber, after went back to sleep another four hours. I really must stop that, sheesh. Anyway, don't mind me just munching on scrumptious kelp being lazy. Wait, did you say sea fan? How will I scratch my back if you remove it?? Best to leave species in its natural element. Not just for my convenience, I promise you."

Litter, jetsam and flotsam wash up daily in the lagoon.

"You're so nifty Magdeline. I'm going on a limb, because of your enormous collection of hooks, you never go hungry, may we checkout your collectibles?"

"Of course you can!" she answered. "Over time, lobstermen have dropped hooks, gloves, buckets, tin cans and more. I can barely keep up! Sometimes I make use of them, mostly not. It makes seagrass taste awful, yuk! Never go near the lobster pot; sailors will trick you, then eat you! Now, a gift for Grand-Lobs, how about an unbreakable glass bottle?"

"Thank you, they are simple walks of life," shared Roe.

'Bloop, Bloop, Bloop...

"Oh, hi!" said Octavia, a dumbo octopus, who is ironically intelligent, wearing charms on her aquatic arms.

"Hello, how did you get inside this bottle?" Magdeline asked her new contortionist neighbor.

"Easy, just moved in from the deep sea! I really needed to see the light; life is too short. Want to help me pick out a shell for my door?"

"Sure, how about this one?!" The limbo lobsters said a few seconds later, wasting no time.

"Thanks, I appreciate your sense of aesthetic style," replied the purple fashionista.

Last night was beyond amusing. Roe can hardly wait to visit the popular 'big' reef, filled with curiosity.

"Good morning twins, I adore the gifts you brought me. What a nice addition to my trinket box. Did you enjoy your time?" asked ambidextrous, fifteen-pound Mama-Rouge.

"Yes, we did!"

"Super! A gift for you too! Delphine the dolphin invited us to the annual lighting' at the reef with singing angelfish."

Bouncing on their tails, they shouted, "Yay, yippee, wahoo we can't wait. Reel in the fun!"

"It's still a week away. Let's prepare for the holidays, maybe sponge clean the house," said Mama-Rouge.

Knock, knock...

"Hey Delphine, just in time! I'm telling the twins about the Coral Reef Festival."

"Ahoy! It smells delicious, what's cooking?! I had to stop by' it reeks from the buoy."

"Seaweed pancakes with fish sauce; let me make you a plate."

"Heck yea, fishier the better," said Delphine, "but they look like tar balls."

The conch shell-cell lights up ringing. Octavia calls the twins over for routine ring toss.

"Fun, meet you after dark," said Roe.

At the lagoon, fluorescent circles are tossed onto her glass habitation.

"Throw me one," shouted Roe, catching it with her antenna.

"Toss me eight," replied Octavia, using octo-legs to partake.

"Wow, you're so talented, think I can do it with my numero' ocho?" asked Twin-Roe, occasionally speaking Latin like her father.

Hours of activity, before dreaming of sunrise.

Another year of winter festivities. Family traditions, hiding barnacles and sea cucumbers in aquatic trees. Cheerful and bright, with fall's aroma moving through the windy night. Although peaceful, Paparoa sensed trouble when ominous sounds echoed, "Grab the stick, we'll scare them out."

Swoosh, swoosh... "Come-in, come-in..."

"Captain speaking, what's good?" he heard.

"Hey guys, did you hear about the blue lobster caught up coast yesterday? Rumor has it, they're traveling south to a marine museum in Key West, Florida. If we hurry, we can make it to the dock in time to get a glimpse; a one in two million chance," lobstermen converse 'toeing the line.'

Waterways clear, no clouds, only blue skies ahead. The lucky men are ready for a big win, without hesitation, and a wide grin. Just then, Roe is awoken from wind of peculiar noises, "What's happening Mama?" she asked.

"Stay back! They're poking at us with a long stick!"

"Got you; you're going to be tasty!" said the wicked man, grabbing Mama-Rouge's tail.

"Over my dead body, take me instead," shouts Paparoa. "I'm tastier with more meat at 20 pounds!"

"Well, well, well... I do have a special license for jumbos like yourself. Hmm, never made a deal like this. Get in the crate..." he telepathically, dreadfully negotiates.

"Please do not let them hurt you," cried Roe.

Lobstermen struggle with Paparoa as he turned around with barely time before disappearing to yell out, "Be right back!" Devastated, unsure of plans and grieving in silence; Roe did not give up, having faith - the size of the ocean.

A misty night with a twinkle of hope. A sign, the show must go on. Difficult to sleep, decorating the cubby hole needed to be complete. Mama-Rouge suggests inviting Octavia and Delphine over to lift my spirits. It did not take long to arrive.

"Hi Twinsies, we're here."

"So happy you made it safely. Please can you lift this off me?"

Octavia spins the ocean greenery amazingly fast, adding shell garland Mama-Rouge had made.

Pier lights reflected off the mini tree as they gather to say a prayer for those lost at sea. Little Roe wishes upon a star as she places a starfish topper atop it. Magdeline swims by with a gift; a sentimental object she found while floating around.

"Here, girls, have these sunglasses lobstermen wear to see clearly."

"Thank you, I'll cherish them - when looking down at the ground," said Roe.

Unaware of special powers they hold, abruptly transferred into a social media time warp when cleaning the mysterious frames. Blurriness turned into picturesque waves, switching to wavelength videos of lobster vessels around the country.

"Where's my expensive shades," said the lobsterman, looking everywhere in a rugged manner, "without them I won't be able to see through the water," realizing they fell off his hat when baiting her father.

Frightened, Roe decides to put them temporarily away.

Later, more obscure sounds muffled from a different boat. Listening closely, men jabbered on walkie-talkies, "Get back to the shore. A storm is on the way; we can't chance losing the prized catch. Pay for this will feed our families for winter."

"I conquer Captain, your way or the Island Express-Way sir."

Roe witnesses trawlers headed for land.

Part Two:

Largo the Lobster

Alongside commercial buoy lines, Paparoa is making way to Key West on a 22ft. Downeast boat. Winds are gaining speed. White caps bigger. Dangerous conditions, and a bumpy ride as lobstermen scattered. A rare, shiny, bright blue lobster is also heading south on board a 'lobster yacht' unknowingly, building strength against strong currents.

Lobster traps are unloaded. Coolers set aside. Confusion is unfolding. Winds are knocking over ice containers causing a distraction, when Paparoa's crate is misplaced on the wrong boat. In the corner, sits a tearful four-inch marvelous lobster.

"Why are you crying little lobby?" asked Paparoa. "It will be alright."

"I was separated from my family in Maine," replied a shaky, soft voice.

"A lengthy trip for your size, no worries! We'll be just fine; I made a promise to return to mine," reassuring, "all we need is safe depth. Ever heard of Mark Twain' ha, never mind. Anyway, my hometown name suits you, Largo."

"Largo? I almost thought you meant to mercilessly cut my tail; a term I recall hearing aboard."

Five in the morning with a few miles to the museum's port, the bearded men set out into rough seas. Wave after unrelenting wave, crashes against the outdated ship.

Lobster traps are tossed side to side. Paparoa remains calm as they sailed the unforgiving sea; inevitably, growing a bond while trying to hang on - for life.

Mama-Rouge investigates the eyewear left at the pier, "He is alive, Paparoa is okay! I must send Slate to his rescue." Mile marker zero, not much further. Dangerous weather did not stop Slate on a mission. Roe checked for updates as he ventures, enlisting Delphine for extra encouragement.

"Hey! I'm here, you got this!" said the dolphin.

"Wasup, I need your speed in order to keep up or we'll lose them," emphasized Slate.

Delphine does not slowdown in turbulent water. Onboard melted ice for almost twenty-four hours, Largo feels dizzy, suffering vertigo; weak from a lack of salinity.

Delphine spots a ship ahead when out of the blue, a huge wave slams into the loaded boat causing lobster trap doors to unlatch. Paparoa and Largo are thrown, sliding toward the sidewall as they slip out drain holes along the deck.

"Hang on! Have no fear, let the sea set you free!" shouted Paparoa, falling to the sea floor, forty feet beneath the Seven Mile Bridge.

Largo sinks, hitting rock bottom - finding his sea legs.

The monsoon has repositioned into a tropical storm. Chilly weather helped Largo adapt to the new climate. Plop' they land on the sea floor where Delphine likes to tailgate, "You're free! Wahoo! Who's tagging along with you?" she asked.

"This is Largo, lost in the serenity, found by the water."

"An exceptional blue lobster if I may say," she replied.

Not one to miss the parade, Paparoa invites the unique marine life to join in celebration.

Courteous Delphine leads the way back in a periwinkle mood. Safeguarding, Slate followed for extra security, not taking any chances endangering precious cargo. Murkiness made navigating difficult. Luckily, the bold shark has vision for miles.

At nightfall, Paparoa learned more about Largo, "So tell me, which high seas do you belong to?"

"I'm from a small harbor, where tourists on a charter noticed my unusual shell jumping with excitement, shouting, "Way to go, we must bring him to the fishery. A blue lobster will bring compensation."

"Tossing a net to sell me to longshore men, who sold me to a vendors café - who sold me again."

"Now it's all making sense," he replied.

The tired lobster is giving up while transported to a maritime museum when rescued, by miracles of sunlight on a cloudy day.

"Keep going Largo, there's more layers to your shell than you imagine! What seems unfair now will be used for another purpose," advised the pioneer father.

Roe anxiously awaits, checking for Paparoa's location. The surf has changed causing swells to blur, "Oh no! I can't see him anywhere! Sand is distorting my vision," she yelps.

"No spazzing out, pipe down to help Mama-Rouge cheer up. We should choose outfits for the show tomorrow night. A total glow up, you might meet someone special," encourages Twin-Roe.

Creative, Roe wears recycled fashion pieces, preferring biodegradables for quick outfit changes.

"Adorable! Except, pier mates are too shallow for me. You sure it's a good idea... guess I might reconsider. No way will I have a family with just any crustacean, unless adventurous, spontaneous, even a little daring!"

"Keep an open mind sis... you will make yourself stir crazy," insisted Twin-Roe.

Paparoa picks up the pace, having deadlines to beat. A few miles to go, the reef radiant with luminous glow. Below the Overseas Highway, festival hosts and residents to the reefs, squid brothers Scuzzy and Scoozy are overseeing, when they receive notice of a distinct creature. Fascinated and slightly pushy, they hope it will make an exciting finale. Audiences align in anticipation of the special guest invited by the sibling attendees in charge.

Energetic, Caribbean reef squid Scuzzy and Scoozy, with big smiles and chartreuse-green bowties, no bigger than an oyster in length reach Largo. Within minutes, the pair having large eyes on each side, see in far range. Waving tentacles, the hyper siblings holler, "Hey, slow down Larry!"

"It's Largo, nice to meet you."

"Same to you, finally, a real gig. We coordinate the show's itinerary each year; please accept this late invite?"

"Sure, except, I'm timid in front of crowds."

"No way, I don't believe that with your natural beauty, you should embrace your differences. If we can make it at one inch, anyone can!"

"Ouch I stubbed my big claw."

"Oh, heck no, are you ok? We don't want to overwhelm or pressure you. We're not the spiteful type," claim Scuzzy and Scoozy.

"That hurt. I'll be there. But please remove the bands from my claws. Super uncomfortable. I'm claustrophobic or as my parents say, "claws-trophobic."

The trio squabble, "Pull this way... pull that way," until the elastic flings off. Largo thanks them for doing him a solid.

"No problem! We're happy to know you can protect us with those bad boys."

"Of course, I owe you both a fishy' dishy!"

Paparoa suggested, "We better keep going, It will be morning soon."

At low tide around 6am, Roe chose to stay in her den. An opportunity to check the photonic lens when a dreary voice is heard, "Oh man, how did this happen? I had superstitious green bands on the claws, an unfortunate catch," lobstermen talked amongst themselves, "better luck next time."

Elated hearing the conversation, no longer somber, "Yippie, Paparoa is near!" Roe shouted.

New Year's Eve. Sealife makes way to the reef in bubbly attire. Mama-Rouge wore her usual shell necklace, shell hat, and shell shoes. Twin-Roes wear scalloped dresses with dazzling iridescent colors.

"Attention all, on your floaties! The aquatic talent show will be starting momentarily," Scuzzy and Scoozy announce the program to begin, "lights, camera, anemone!"

One by one, they display quirky abilities. In line, first, the four-eyed fish able to see above and below water. Then, a bunch of colorful hues flaunted by the parrot fish. Next up, rockstar of the reef, the large hump head wrasse jams out to fifteen minutes of fame. Lastly, the leafy sea dragon, expert at camouflaging a graceful glide. Roe searches for Paparoa as crowds applaud. Giant windflowers make it difficult to see past audience.

Eves countdown begins. Ten, nine, eight, seven... Scuzzy and Scoozy shew Largo with instructions, "It's time, claw your way to the top - rock, surprise the crowd!" Unprepared in a scurry, Paparoa reminds him, "Be creative, you will do beyond great, a piece of sponge cake. Ignore that, something the market baker would say to OG-Lob."

Crowds cheer, as Largo climbed atop the rock to reveal his blue shell through Octavia's fancy bubble maker.

In true form, he astonished the guests with his signature one claw break dance. Roe was in shock at the swagger in his tail; her mooneyes sparkled in a daze. A magnetic force washed over, as if time had stood still in that moment. Unaware, more adventures await.

"Papa, you kept your promise."

"Sure did! I told you this year's resolution is to roll with the tides' my little crustaceans," he continued, "my word is my blood, thicker than this water. Meet Largo, headed to where phenomenal marine life is held, who anglers were merciful to his delicate meat."

"I'm aware! Someone has lost their eyewear, an undiscovered portal to land and sea. Allowing me to track all your nautical whereabouts."

"A miracle we're reunited, the rest is water under the bridge. Let's make Largo feel welcomed," said Paparoa.

"Live the salt life with us bro." Scuzzy and Scoozy offered residency on the reef, "It will be cool having you around."

Twin sisters, Largo and crewmates participate in the 'Shore Protection Program' for polluted goods, avoiding dangers. Close buddies, Octavia, and Delphine join the exploration. At sundown, Roe curiously roamed to the reef's other side, "Yikes, my tail's stuck in a plastic bag! It's getting late, Mama-Rouge will worry," she wept trying to free herself.

After dark, Slate swims his nightly surveillance routine, "Roe, is that you tangled in rubbish?" he asked. "Wait for me to get help."

"Yes, S.O.S. please!"

Slate locates the group, "Roe is in danger, you can save her with your claws before she suffocates or ends up lobster bait." Divers are out on Saturdays. Largo moves quick.

"Hold up! It's a busy weekend. If they see a lobster, you may end up 'soup du jour on tomorrow's menu," dares Paparoa.

"That's disgusting, I won't let you down," he said stunned, followed by bumping tails, a way of showing high regard. Slate, known to be the ocean realtor, controls divers on his property. He swims ahead to inform Roe that rescue is on the way, "We're here, don't panic!"

Largo is instructed to use his main claw, crusher, and pincher to rip the plastic.

On scene, Scuzzy and Scoozy gripped the trash bag with long tentacles. Largo cuts as Roe breaks free - having each's back.

"Impressive, see you around," she said blushing.

By days end, confident he can tackle any obstacle, even love.

Playing hard to catch is Roe's stronger attribute as she matured. All fun and games until, love tapped.

"Hey, what was that for?!" asked confused Largo.

"Because, uh... I will explain later," she said in dashing style, leaving behind a fragrance surely to attract. Slate reminded him, "Relationships can be rocky; you must be a trustworthy friend first."

"Challenge accepted," he answered taking a risk.

Under the sea, sibling squids help prepare Largo for the upcoming Valentines day, teaching him charismatic phrases of the waterways.

"You're ready for a date!"

"Thanks dudes, your support encourages our foundation to grow and sustain."

Following her pheromones... Roe is worth the wager.

Largo is not the only one immersed in thought. At the pier, Roe and Mama-Rouge chat, "Daydreaming about the date has my stomach in knots."

"That is ridiculous, I remember when your father and I had our first date. It was difficult to see him with blurry vision; we rely heavily on intuition. They have similar characteristics, such as brave and inconspicuous. You'll dig it."

The moon subtle. Roe sees bashful Largo.

"You're striking," he compliments.

"Am I salty for not liking surprises?" she asked.

"Not at all, given people like to invade our personal space."

"Then why are you changing color??"

"Ahh, what... um...I think it's my attraction for you," he said, turning darker blue.

A time of leisure, as they sat on the rocky ledge by a flickering lighthouse. "It's been fun catching shrimp with you. Want to meet next high tides and do it again?" he asked glancing at each other after every bite.

"Two sand buckets of shrimp will surely make you sea-sick," she gushes in return.

"You're right, not sure I can eat anymore," he said with a full belly. The night continued with exchanges of laughter. Roe's inquisitive nature leads to discovering more about her blue crushes background, "I have a way for you to catch up, check these out."

Largo zoomed closely at the sunglasses with mystical powers.

A seemingly well-dressed Captain, owner of a café stand, is expecting a large seafood order.

Gazing into the lens, a heinous laugh appeared, "Hahahaha... where is my blue lobsta?! I need my medicine!"

"Do you ever see your entourage?" she inquired, watching him quiver from the video.

"I was born in a tourist area where my family still lives for amusement, if only they knew I'm alive."

Roe extends a reassuring hug with long limbs, "There might be a way to find them with this aqua net, look again, what do you see?"

On screen, in a prism of colors, the insane man vents, "Bahahaha, where the heck is my one pounder?? Watch me boil him alive, I'm sick like that!" snarks, the restauranteur.

In a panic, Largo begins to tailspin.

"Is everything ok?" asked Roe.

"Yes, okay with us, except I must go. I recognize that man's laugh. He's the owner of the Po'boy stand where my adopted parents are kept. He's planning a seafood bake back home. They saved me for some time, now I must save them."

"Wait, before you go... um... will you be my blue lobster if I don't see you after this?" Largo disappeared without a trace. Instead, focusing on the upcoming Maine Lobster Race.

The intrepid to save his family will be a tough, yet necessary decision to make. Mama-Rouge, in a chic accent, asks "How did the date go?"

"It was perfect! Except you have the 'go' part right; he had to leave for now. I hope to see him," she uttered painfully, knowing it may not be soon.

"Surely, he won't forget you. He may admire your perfume named 'True Love' – wait for his shell-call."

In a salty mood, Roe retreats to bed, powerless to sleep. Once again, relying on the fisheye lens as a compass for loved ones offshore.

On a shipwrecked reef, Largo is courageously, unsuccessfully tying cord to driftwood using his pinchers. Roe monitors the screen when he is seen capsizing on the floating debris.

Slate plans to accompany the shellfish up coast. Portal lens shows him losing to the bitter end of the rope. Mama-Rouge suggests they find something thrifty to assist along the way or ask Magdeline for something laying around.

"Oh no... woah... woah... woosh, why do I keep falling off. I'm so tired of this!" blurts Largo.

Making way, Slate moves towards the coral using incredible senses, and common sense.

"You won't be able to go alone, unless you want to arrive late for the total eclipse," he said.

"Well excuse you, Mr. shark, pardon those lips!"

During the summer, bull sharks adapt to weather conditions of northern temperatures.

"Why are you picking on me? Is it my delicacy your palette craves?" conveys, fragile Largo.

"Ha! A misunderstanding, I'm allergic to shellfish. It's how Paparoa and I remain good friends," adding, "Magdeline has a diver's flipper to get you there quicker."

Largo hops onto the piece of wooden wreckage as Slate pulls him to where Magdeline snored loudly from afar. Extra careful not to disturb the sea cow.

Restless, Octavia squeezes supremely out of her home, "So many bubbles," she said.

"Glad you're here. I'm not trying to burden your neighbor, but we have an issue and need a favor," responded Largo.

"No prob! It's my job to resolve entangled scenarios," replied Octavia, always giddy and witty.

"May we use the diver's shoe from scrappage?"

"Of course, I'm in charge of the overnight shift!"

Octavia began tossing collectibles, some clean - others rustier, not so pristine.

"Found it, be safe - bon voyage!!"

Slate prefers the scenic route. Switching gears, Largo stepped into the best means of transportation. Slate picked up the maturing five-inch lobster by the flipper's heel, who needed to solely believe in himself. This is all it took to brave the excursion.

"Staying close to shorelines has less risk," said Slate, "besides, who'd bully you next to this pirate? There's no trying that tuna business on us. Whoever 'tail-ropes' me is getting pulled in."

"Exactly why I like going places with you," replied Largo.

Hours in, set adrift, forgetting the task while rambling about Roe.

"Elongated arms scratching my back, perfume that smells of sea breeze, antennas of tactile defensiveness..."

Slate preferred singing tunes when maneuvering, "Life takes us on unexpected turns, so keep prevailing earthling," he said, looking at his missing fin, "this is why they call me a pirate."

"That makes two of us, when I lose one," agreed Largo.

"How about I share my favorite shanty song, it may help,"

Slate sings in a rhotic accent...

"Arrgh, we ever prepared enough...,

Is there ever a way to keep up...,

Arrgh, we ever prepared enough...,

No, no, no...,

Chomp, Chomp, Chomp...,

Arrgh, we ever prepared enough...,

Arrgh, we able to stay up past dusk...,

No, no, no...,

Chomp, Chomp, Chomp...,

Carry on... carry on... carry on...,

Arrgh, we ever prepared enough...,

No! We're never ready enough...,

Chomp!"

Lifeguards warned beachgoers of a shark lurking in the area. Numerous reports made to rescue towers for miles north.

Cruising Florida's turquoise waters allow for clarity and soaking it all in. Largo is snug in tow, with his Maine claws over the flippers' front. If Slate went slow, Largo signals to keep going.

Time is on their side. No predators to attack, no anglers to fear; a sunny day with all perfectly intact. It was to change at a popular fishing pier, where tourists toss scraps attracting life below. Passing through without a trace, or at least they hoped. Reaching the other side, a pier attendant shouts, "Lobster in shark's mouth!"

Patrons scurry for a glimpse of the outlandishness, unable to witness any action, walking away disappointed. The attendee on deck was able to snap a photo in time, posting a video that goes viral overnight.

Unbothered, Largo and his smooth co-pilot have become a media sensation. Gliding through the dark night, making it to Virginia Beach. Further north, seaside temperatures mark the halfway point. Roe daydreams in Florida, pausing for a status update on her beau, while Largo secures family upstate.

In Maine, po'boy vendor known locally as Captain Wry-fi, is frying lobster hoagies when the phone dings; a trendy video in his news feed of a rare lobster causes him to forget his sizzling meal. The café ignites into a huge cloud of smoke. In the heated moment, he grabs two pet lobsters out of the tank, frantically tossing them in a pail; he ran to the splintered boondocks.

Chef watches as his beloved business burned to the ground. Crushed by the incident, he cries for all to hear, "Oh no, now I'm just a po'boy! What will I do?? I'm calling Captain Laiz, pronounced l-i-e-s; he has nothing better to do." "Hey Brother, what are you and Mrs. Waverly up too?"

"Not much, was just thinking of you."

"Great! Tell your wife to pack a suitcase, you're needed here. We're going to catch my famed bait embarking to Florida with a cash reward, according to channel 28. The log cabin can wait."

Maintaining virtue and wearing a black and white bougee bib, his adored tourist site burst into flames. Without direction and shallow pockets, options were slim. In a pinch, Capt. Laiz fly's from Rhode Island to Maine in attempts to save his brother from financial disaster.

Frightened, Roe dropped the sunglasses that wedged between rocks, losing power when the lens scratch. Upset by this, thinking to herself...'better left at sea, if meant to be, he will retrace his steps returning to me.'

Instead of treading lightly, Roe began a new hobby of shucking clams. Mama-Rouge teaches how to make seafood paella, a favorite of Paparoa's, hoping to someday impress Largo. Determined to be a self-taught cook, she inevitably is faced with more challenges.

Dangerous temperatures in Summer, causes sea-pansies to bleach to colorless toxins. Making matters worse, OG-Lob has fallen ill to a bad reaction of coral dermatitis one week after burying Grandma-Lob, who passed at one hundred and five years old from exhaustion.

Overwhelmed, creature of habit retreated, not to re-emerge until days later. Tough love from fraternal twin, who tells her sibling, "Enjoy a sponge-bath spa day." Advising to push on with activities and natural remedies, like night swims. Always reliable advice, except Largo was still on her mind, extremely worried about his vulnerability to people and predators, hoping for his safe voyage upon return. In a way, waiting for him helped heal the heartache of losing Grandma-Lob.

At the shipyards, Largo and Slate are in shock to see the sky erupt in flames, like a picture resembling the Fourth of July. "Take us close to the dockside," requests, co-pilot Largo with much aptitude.

Captain Wry-fi, wearing an apron and chef hat, holds rope attached to a mop bucket. Moving closer, Largo goes out of water to confirm the familiar face.

"Be safe, I will be low-key chilling here," said Slate.

Carefully, he climbs pilings as chef sobbed in a slumber sitting on the dock. Largo sees his parents distressing inside the cracked leaking pail, "Son, is it really you? We've missed you! How did you find us? Did someone put a geographical tracker on you?"

Greeting in a rush not to be seen, he replies, "Ma', Pa' it's me, we're safe; a long story."

His parents warn, "Careful not to wake chef or consider us fried fritters."

Largo whispered, "Hold tight while I cut ties, my confidant is taking us to safety."

Avoiding dangers back to Florida is top priority. Midnight waters further out to sea are the chosen routes not made hastily. The internet video circulates, attracting unwanted attention. Offshore, sitting in close quarters, they introduce one another, "A gentle giant with a slightly temperamental side. No reason to freak out, a likable foe, making it easy to co-exist," said Largo of Slate.

"Thank you for rescuing us. That man's laugh almost broke the glass, we always knew you were a dependable son."

"There's little worry in the company of good fins," Slate assured them.

Heading further south, restraints are removed from his parent's claws. Largo announced he has met someone special, when asked why they are enroute to a faraway destination.

Finally, across the sea, a beam of dim light is seen. Arrival at last. Largo expresses gratitude to his thick-headed pal before departing, making sure his parents are accommodated with shelter at the reef. He dashes off to find Roe.

Along the way, in the bay, Delphine and Magdeline are asleep taking power naps. Octavia is awake, playing the game Mo'fishy-fishy with sea urchin neighbors, flipping cups and large pebbles.

A few rocks below, sitting quietly in her thoughts, Roe remembers a familial motto 'saltwater cures all wounds.'

"Hey there, Cheer up!" said Largo, surprising her, presenting a heart-shaped shell he found on his trek. Roe embraces him, ecstatic he is back in town.

"You always make my feet go clickity-clack, clickity-clack," said, the love struck hearty red lobster.

"Great idea let's move and groove. It helps my mood!" Largo flaunts nifty breakdancing skills, like when they first met.

Twirling, curling until morning, huddled closely under his jumbo, her heartbeat went, pitter-patter... pitter-patter.

Intimate arrangements made for the families to meet. Good friends, Scuzzy and Scoozy extend sand dollars or tickets, to dinner and a spectacle at the Keel Over Comedy Theater. It lit up with slugs, smudging straight and narrow paths of fluorescent colors across the stage. Squid siblings entertain, "Woah, who put me on the menu?" they asked. "Please, no ordering fried calamari dinner!" The group dine on Octavia's specialty of seaweed salad and ink noodles from her ancestors. Somehow, carrying an ink-sac with tricks up her sleeve.

After a night out, Largo is smitten when he asks reserved Roe for another date.

"For shore! In return, would you retrieve my goggles?"

"I got you," he said.

Without hesitation, the glossy blue creature reached for the polarized portal, "Ouch, I'm stuck!"

"Hang on, I got you too!" Roe wrapped her limbs around his tail, lifting him up with all her might.

Trying her best to free him when a large rock falls, crushing a crucial claw. In shock, Roe swiftly checks for injury.

"I'm okay, it felt like a snap, crunch, and a tear - no big deal. Besides, there's more where they came from."

"You always make me laugh," she said flirting.

The misfit squids successfully lift the bolder, retrieving lobster-lands gateway. Nurturing Roe brings bandages and soft sponges for his wounds. Selflessness captured the heart of Largo, winning his affection.

Friends gather for a game of 'Largo Solo' where eyes are shut to seek each other, unexpectedly, finding an oyster; testing the strength of his claw and extra small limbs. Pulling it apart, to discover a lavish opaque pearl, or as Mama-Rouge says, "Luxurious." In amazement, he keeps it discreet.

"Largo, Solo... Largo... got you trapped!" Roe said, fluttering her eyes and a squeeze of endearment.

Over time, the lobsters grew into more. A tried-and-true relationship deserved a larger pearl; not hesitating with plans to double its size, working diligently manipulating the gem. Spinning and tumbling the silverish nature made stone, until it collected debris, taking on extraordinary shape. Exquisitely polished for honest intentions through calming or rough waters.

Largo had waited for the right moment, to unveil his unfeigned emotions. Visiting with Paparoa first was a sign of respect. Contemplating options, he paces, knowing family approval is crucial for their communal success. Accepting Largo was a tropical breeze, "An ideal mate for my daughter," Paparoa extends valued blessings.

Largo, reassured he is making the right decision, turns tail toward the reef, "Catch you later!" he shouts.

"Let's hope not!" replied Paparoa.

Halfway there, Slate swims by rattling the five-inch lobsters' millions of nerves.

"Hey, you know it freaks me out when I see a sneaky shadow. I almost seize."

"I thought you could use a bite of security, considering you have no other defense at the moment."

Largo appreciates the goodwill, thanking him for not being shady.

Part Three:

Marriage of Largo & Roe

The ten-foot shark idled at a comfortable pace, keeping up easy, for a friend with boosted adrenaline.

“You seem happy, what’s the occasion?” asked Slate.

“I found my life mate,” replied Largo.

The places chemistry takes you, never hesitate.

Incomprehensible, the flirtatious shark tries to convince him otherwise, "For life? Sounds fishy, love bites. There's plenty of lobsters in the Keys."

"Except only one for me," insisted Largo.

"Well then, we can have you married this holiday weekend with everyone on deck. Is it too soon?"

"Of course not. There is something different about her, like a pocket full of sunshine," said Largo, "not a bad idea, you're not so grey like they say.

"If there's a will, there's a wave to lead the way," claims Slate.

A proper micro-wedding before mini lobster season on the list of priorities. Largo and Roe spent time apart due to harsh wind and rough seas, leaving both uneasy, like a hollow empty exoskeleton.

Skys cleared, Roe asked Paparoa if her scratched plastics were repairable. Attempting to fix them, the distorted screen still has content showing different scenarios.

A group of people seen out for dinner ordering 'surf-n-turf' humor themselves. A patron tells a realistic joke in a biting tone, "Three species at the dining table, share a nine-month pregnancy... a woman, cow, and a lobster."

Switching videos, doomed restauranteur is speaking to his insurance agent on a landline. In a random, loud outburst, not knowing whether to laugh or cry, he sighs, "My dreams went up in smoke, my po'boy stand is gone!! I'm sailing away 'seven feet under the keel. This place ruined my whole life, bahaha ha-ha, I should've never bought it! All because of that blue lobsta!"

Swiping again, campground staff enlightens classmates about a lobster locals are on the lookout for, offering anyone who returns it a generous reward, sending Roe into a frenzy. A boy is listening with empathy.

The pier is lit up with patriotic colors, representing a celebration of freedom.

Hours tick-tock by, unable to get sleep. Largo also helplessly awake next to the mother of pearl, compelled to express his admiration for Roe. Grabbing the gem securing it tightly, he set off into the night.

On way to awaken her, caught in a torrential downpour, delaying his proposal, he is unwilling to accept a raincheck.

Tropical rainstorms made peaceful drizzling sounds of tranquility, reminding Largo to remain steadfast through choppy waters, arriving to the pier at five in the morning. Roe hears tapping on her sea glass window. Holding back her smile, she raced to the frosted door.

Always on time, never having anyone wait, an admirable trait. Beautifully, cautiously designed, yet willing to take risks to follow fate.

"Take a walk with me to see the sunrise. I know a spot with incredible views," he said.

"Now? I'm in bed," she hesitates, afraid to abandon the ocean-front house.

"It's okay, we can be out of water up to 24 hours on a cool summer night. Advice your papa taught me."

She trusts him, reaching above the rocks, a beautiful scenery awaits.

Lightning illuminates the sky; a cruise ship goes by twinkling in the distance. Largo embraces Roe, gazing at the stars, he asked, "Will you take the plunge with me?."

"What? Plunge into the water. Terrible idea!"

"Not like that silly shelly! Remember you asked if I would be your blue lobster, and I darted off? Well, like that... will you be my Maine lobster? Marry me?" he asked placing the heavy gem on her tiny pincher.

She accepted, "It's stunning! Although, I hope it stays put," she said, "you are truly one in a million."

An island wedding, enhanced with magical over-the-top fireworks adding to the matrimony.

The moon's eclipse in the background is a perfect backdrop. Without warning, someone double sneezes, then a camper's lantern turns on. Carefully climbing down, unnoticed, they part ways.

"See you later boo-berry, be safe!" said smitten Roe.

"Thank you for believing in me, not colorblind to my shell," replied Largo.

"Still, with your flawed claw and all that mumbo gumbo... I admire you."

Unusual for the reserved spiny lobster to stay out late at night, her grounded sister Twin-Roe, dives deeper for info, "Like, I get that you're nocturnal, but you never stay out late, what's going on?!"

"A magical night. I'm getting married with only a couple of days to prepare for a wedding spectacular!"

"What, are you serious?? I'm down. The most fun day ever, a real lobster extravaganza!! Our band will bring the recycled instruments," said mate of honor, overjoyed and going a little overboard.

Twin-Roe understood the assignment, enlisting the help of reclusive hermit crabs, collectively spending the day to find Rose-petal tellin' shells for invitations. Mama-Rouge stops by to ask Magdeline if she would design a gown using her collectibles. Ecstatic, she gladly unboxes random found tchotchkes.

"Hmm...we have a piece of clear vinyl, white lace, and fishing net...wow, with draping shells... gorgeous!"

Worried, she may be too slow, Octavia offers lending arms. Hours later, it was finally achieved; a disastrous dress turned masterpiece. Mama-Rouge and Roe stopped by for a fitting. Her five-inch tail tailored true-to-size, with a veil to match, a quintessential keepsake.

Delighted, Roe thanks Magdeline and Octavia for their time, talent, and generosity.

Inspired, deciding to craft herself heels and a purse from micro-plastics that have washed upside the pier. An endless night of sewing when it dawned on her… what to give Largo. So, she asked Magdeline for her opinion.

The borderline hoarder, in a neat-effective way, offers to gift the groom a gem she has been saving in her treasure chest, "Have this, something blue, an aqua marine diamond. Mama-Rouge can craft a necklace for him in case he was to crack another claw, and that's not much of a ring on you if it falls off. You will need a lobster clasp, or strings attached."

"If you think so, sure! I will wear mine as a necklace too, thank you!"

"Also, something found, a white cloth bowtie, ha' love never fails," said the well-rounded manatee.

"Absolutely perfect!!"

As boats arrive for mini season, both lobster families hightail it into gear in preparation for the wedding. Twin-Roe assigns crew roles before dinner rehearsal held at the reef, halfway to the exclusive island.

A pile of gifts sits. Paparoa gave a father of the bride speech, "Today we celebrate the stamina it took to get here. Battling seas, escaping fisheries, and avoiding pollutants to name a few. Living in a small community on the same accord is not easy, sometimes even tricky. In the end, it's acceptance of our individuality that brings us in unity. Love is a powerful, and complex emotion. Most of all, cheers to the future heir to the pier."

Mama-Rouge causes a wake by having the last word, "Give me cotton candy grand-lobbies!"

The party laughed at an uncanny possibility of it happening.

As night falls, guests elegantly arrive for Delphine's shuttle service to the ceremony, two hundred feet from the pier.

Magdeline and Delphine closely coordinate through flashy shell-cells, communicating mostly forecasted hurricanes, or other emergencies like struck by a boat.

Early to rise, Magdeline calls her bottled nose cousin, "Top of the morning to you cuz! I'm fishing for last minute details while still daylight. With your help, we can have the festivity setup by the time Largo and Roe awaken."

"That's flippin' great - on my way!" said Delphine. "Hey friends, is anyone prepared yet? I wrote a song for the couple in case you're late. Do you want to hear it?!" Octavia prepares a rhythm, managing to avoid ripple effects.

"Oh hi, I didn't see you camouflaged. What's on your mind? Where do you want me?" asked Delphine. "Give me a second to get my bubble machine working, we're waiting for Twin-Roe to orchestrate everything properly," said the delicate, outgoing octopus.

"Alright, gather around like usual. Octavia sings, I'm on the snorkel flute. Scuzzy and Scoozy on percussion, with milk cartons and extra straw mallets. Delphine is on the whistle. Magdeline, you're red cup clapping - absolutely no foam," Roe's sister delegates.

Slate gives a follow up demonstration, "Ready, put your claws and flippers out. Swing left, then right - spinning around with souls in flight."

A time to unwind with no flaws in sight, ready for the big night! Per request on a salvaged microphone, Octavia began.

The clever octopus sings, not skipping a beat...

"Floating out at sea...,
I have my lobby here with me...,
She said, "Stay with me...,
Lucky, lucky me...,
We're feeling bubbly...,
No clouds, all clout...,
No time to pout... the rest is history...,
We're going to have a party...,
Way out at sea with the only one for me...,
An island par-a-r-r-ty...,
Yippie!
Wahoo to my crew!!"

"So, what do you think?"

"It's fantastic, you're a live one!" said friends.

Crewmembers search for white seaweed at sandbanks with extrovert horseshoe-crab community, setting up decorative ornamentation where they horsey-back to get the job done.

The day was sunny with calming wavelets . A sailboat named 'Lobsta-Mobsta, Capt. Wry-fi is beached. Delphine signals Cousin Magdeline, warning of dangerous company when rumors reach Largo who sticks with commitments; a strength instilled in him since birth. The mature blue lobster also acquired a cautious side, beside heedful Roe. Trusting in his gut, knowing 'still waters run deep.'

Carrying on, Magdeline floats by belly side up with a sloppy smorgasbord of essential nutrients and minerals, such as sardines, anchovies, and gelatin shrimp salad - no use for cutlery.

In anticipation, enormous crab colonies place the decorative seaweed across sand in a heart-shape formation.
Catching a lift, misfits, Scuzzy and Scoozy have something to say, "Get outta town, not literally but really, what a beautiful island to get married at, just lovely. Make it a double round, they totally deserve it! A honeymoon for two."

Along for the ride, Octavia is careful not to burn out in the heat, settling for bed where 'sand meets the water.'
In the distance, Captain Wry-fi organizes a table of sparklers. As tide rises, Delphine escorts the party on seated cushion to 'Palm Island, arriving at a beauteous beach. Largo's parents are dumbfounded by the difference in beauty, mentioning, "We've never seen anything like it; you would think we live under a rock."

Delphine returned for the bride. Paparoa, Mama-Rouge and Roe sprung onto the boater's mat. Short rides left extra time for last minute shuttles. Starfishes lined both sides through the pathway of dunes for an unveiling of her long shell-veil. Moments later, stepping out of mirrored water to captivated Largo.

The night is going as arranged, sparks fly. Shells adorned the dress with whimsical clinking sounds. Tunnel vision as she stood before him, hearts pounding; Roe turned deeper red. Along the seashore, half out of water, vows were exchanged, as the backbone to their home of caviar dreams.

Nearby, Captain Wry-fi is never unplugged. First mate Mrs. Wits, and brother Captain Laiz with his wife Mrs. Waverly, celebrate the independence day. The dark sky kindles with fireworks by water's edge.

Next to swaying palm trees and crisp fresh air, ravishing Roe married jaunty Largo; easy to forget, being outside the ocean for long was an illogical idea. Together holding claws, they take a dip - solidifying a pledge of devotion.

Slate circles the island, monitoring the scenic view. Mrs. Wits is seen wading with camera in hand when she notices the lobsters. In disbelief, she shouted to her other half, "Hun, you're never going to believe it."

"What did you find??" he hollers back.

"Red and blue lobsters are tying the knot!"

"What?! What knot we talking about? Not my boat; where's the net?" he cackles. "Bahaha-ha, I always catch and release, you mad?"

"No, you dimwit, look over there."

The captain is moving closer in Largo's direction, missing by a tail.

Unaware of security, Slate and Crab-dad, trolling, while also suspiciously patrolling.

"Hey! I see you looking at my legs," said islander, Crab-dad.

"No, he's looking at their tail," disputes Crabby baby.

"You're right, get em! Full send off the island!"

The crab mob surround the sailboat, simultaneously, lifting the ship further out to sea. Slate gives a hefty push, warning, "Get lost lobster mobster!"

Delphine agrees, "No, no, no... you need to go, go, go... your ship has sailed!"

"Ah, dang, this is insane," said Capt. Laiz, "see what happens when I follow my relative."

"Its fine sweetie, you're doing the right thing," replied Mrs. Waverly.

"Okay, but if we're staying here, I'm buying a houseboat; no negotiating."

"That's right, full throttle ahead, knock them' dead," she said.

"Babe, this is why I can't live without you; you always think with your head."

Back on shore, the celebration resumed.

"That was epic," said Scuzzy and Scoozy, who are balancing handmade gifts for the newlyweds on Octavia.

"Our gift is our presence," squid brothers said.

"A little heavy, that's enough," said Octavia who gifts first, "Here you go, a message in a bottle... never lose your footing."

Written on scraps is 'Forevermore on Shore.'

The hitch official with an exception, forgoing the kiss instead, sealing with a tender pinch. Everyone watched them sacredly toss the bottle into the ocean.

From Magdeline, a conch shell displayed beautifully in the sand as a good luck charm. Delphine has an anchor wishing marital longevity. Slate gifts a large shark tooth; a reminder he always has their back. The moon glistened with reflections of symbolism. A tropical hideaway of coconuts.

Time to regroup from the wild destination wedding. Largo scoops Roe with his single claw, carrying her to the pier.

Once there, dock crabs align bopping up and down in a timely manner. A farewell to another lobster generation.

Part Four:

Heir to the Pier

A lightning storm has begun. Newly married, working hard on attaining stability to start a family.

“Bring your tail here and cuddle me,” said Largo. Spending quality time together, he and Roe prepare for a Lil’ roux or possibly two, maybe more, three or even - four.

The Florida lobster crawled out of her shell to procreate with barely any uninterrupted time together. The peace was soon to disappear when instigators, Scuzzy and Scoozy stopped by to chat, having tentacles in other's business.

"Largo, are you for real, you're leaving the reef and relocating to the stinky pier??" They asked, expressing frustration and rejection, questioning if they have been replaced.

"Where did you hear that?"

"Uh, just a rumor somebody told someone, who told us."

Confused, not to be hurtful, charming Largo is careful what to say, "Okay, I'm out! Mother nature has new plans for me."

Caught off guard, and visibly upset, they argue, "So, you're going to leave your best friends just like that? The nerve of you, kick rocks! That's something a sea roach would do!"

"Well, goobers, I'm not going far. Stop over-reacting, you're being dramatic! Plus, you two make a good team yourselves. Reminding them, "We will still be at Club-Ocean cleanup on Saturday."

"Pesch, what a dude. The struggle is real," whispering to each other - on hidden reefs of selfish pride.

"He has a point; it does take lobsters forever to start a family. They need quality time, we should go."

"I haven't left yet," Largo chuckles, "be cool."

Giving back is important to Largo and Roe. Keeping waters clean meant a tremendous amount for the survival of aquatic life. Having been welcomed by all with gracious hospitality, Largo felt it necessary to accompany Roe. At the same time, a lively group of sea campers gear up to snorkel. While scavenging around trash and thingamajigs, Magdeline overhears the staff telling students, "If you see the esteemed lobster, film it on your 'go-flow' camera to win a tumbler for second place, and a fishing pole for first."

One by one, water splashes as they hop off a pontoon boat. Magdeline warns sea friends, "We have visitors accompanied by tour guides searching for Largo."

A newly conceived Roe is submerged by it all. Without hesitation, Largo builds a fortress to believe in, an elaborate rock castle, aka Rockas. The bottom dwelling families reside in separate headquarters.

It held strong and sturdy, like concrete against crashing waves, proving to be a reciprocated relationship. Adding a metal hook for Roe's spectacles to hang, displaying skillful agility and inventiveness with his singular claw. Taking little time to complete, excelling in speed.

Worn out, needing a break, entailed to check the portal. Captain Wry-fi demanded that his wife not post a video of navigational coordinates, scheming to be the one to win.

"I'm not going anywhere. Took me ten days to sail from Maine; this reward is mine! I lost him once, not again, bahaha. I will buy a new sidewalk café, one even better than before!" said the mischievous man.

Displeased, Mrs. Wits threatens her husband with darkness of the internet, "Honey, either change your latitude' attitude or I press send."

Captain's plans have gone awry, complaining of spoiled food, hangry for more options, "Look at this crap we're eating! Throw these darn hot dogs away, they're making me sick! Been out here three days in this scorching heat, could have been four, bahaha - I'm sick of it!"

"Calm down, your brother's in town. I'm sure he will make your favorite crab cakes or fish and chips," Mrs. Wits replied.

Staying awake, Roe taps the lens; campers are on way to lunch. Classmate, Giacomo chases a coconut as it tumbled to the pier's end, landing in the water, "Oh no, come back here coconut!" he shouted in the wind.

Reaching for it, he knocked off the rockas' roof, exposing vulnerable Largo, "Whoa, it's you so cleverly hidden! I won't sabotage you, you're remarkable," he said forgetting the fruit.

Science teacher Ms. Manners, also counselor on duty, called for Giacomo, "Class is waiting, what is so interesting? Please enlighten us."

"Ahh, my coconut fell in."

"Well, hmm, then join your peers, we haven't got all day to waste. We should be studying the ocean's plankton through a microscope," she said with discipline.

Spending the day in wonder, pondering his encounter with the blue lobster. Each morning, Giacomo visits his new acquaintance, concerned for his wellness.

"In case you didn't know, there are people hunting for you; you're notorious! Not sure that's a good thing buddy," said Giacomo. "I will protect you."

"Yea I get the gist. Thank you for the reminder, just kidding," replied Largo.

Giacomo asked his classmate to help lift heavy metal signage knocked over on the ground, which read: 'No Docking, No Fishing, No Swimming' placing it back in its proper spot, next to the rock castle. Taking extra measures to ensure the lobster family know their heads, from their tails - never held captive.

The gift of human kindness and compassion surprised Largo, putting him at ease in uncharted waters, while he effortlessly rearranges the exposed Rockas' in the company of expectant Roe without worry.

Thousands of tiny eggs or Lil' roux are due spring of next year. The majority will not stay close to home. Delphine, amused by a drifting coconut, is wildly tossing it in the air until it splits in half, surprising her with refreshing coconut water. The class is entertained by the porpoise showing off quirky tricks with the coconut shell and a half-deflated beach ball; one heavy, one not at all.

Sunset glimmers a mirage. Captain Wry-fi, anchored in the distance is moving toward land in a two-person dinghy, idly coasting along the side, he is careful not to puncture the inflatable boat on pier rocks. Giacomo nervous, looks on as drama unfolds.

"Alright class, in line," said Ms. Manners.

Students request more time, "Can we stay awhile longer?"

"Okay, until sunset," agreed, the warm-hearted teacher.

Ignoring signs, tying up anyway, Capt. Wry-fi docks, "I go where I want, that's who I am! All I need is ice, I'll be quick," he said in a snarky, predictable twang.

Exiting the boat, seeing a blue critter in his peripheral vision, "Wait a second, what do we have here? Ha, I found you! One claw!? Is this some kinda sick joke?? You're coming with me!" he stated, as Largo reconstructs his home.

"I only fish when I'm catching, when I'm catching a lobster dish!" he adds to his delusion, laughing hysterically.

Giacomo recognizes something is wrong shouting, "Put him down, stop bullying the little guy!"

"Who are you ocean whisperer? Mind your own business."

"It is my business; it's everyone's business. Are you a goldfish without self-control, accepting every flake?" asked Giacomo, "why do you want him? Seems greedy."

"I'm not scared of no filthy lobster; more like, he's scared of me! Bahaha!" he continued yapping, "I threw them all back; I didn't keep the fishies', but I keep you!"

Puzzled, Ms. Manners asked, "Is everything alright?"

"No mam, the famous blue lobster lives here, neither out of mind nor out of sight," replied, agitated Giacomo.

Gossip travels fast. Fish and Wildlife Conservationists arrive on scene to check licenses. The lobster mobster has left his identification on board the ship.

"This is a warning! Tread lightly," commands Officer.

"Aye' Aye Captain! Whatever floats your boat!"

"Keep it up, and I'll impound yours. How's that?"

Clamor and chaos have caught the attention of local news.

Checking the seaboard, journalists curiously asked the boy, "Why so uninterested in a trophy?" Picking his battles wisely, he replied firmly with conviction from his inner spirit animal, sprinter of the sea with a king's legacy - the famed lobster, tail.

"People and animals on land, sea, or flying high above trees, deserve to be free with dignity. This is home where the heart beats, not on display or sacrificed on a plate," said Giacomo, requesting reward money be donated to habitat rescue and rehabilitation centers.

Viewers tuned in as the boy makes an impactful statement.

"Okay folks, live from the news, our future marine biologist has no doubt defined his wishes. Stay tuned for the fate of these exquisite souls, off we go."

As promised, Slate always on time, senses danger a mile away. Chomp, chomp, chomp... he takes a bite out of the sinking dinghy.

"That shark devoured my boat!" Captain Wry-fi wailed as it deflates, leaving a buoy and rope floating.

Mrs. Wits calls for him, "Honey, do you need a lifeline?"

Glancing over at a voice so bitter and distasteful, he decides it is time to quit.

"Don't you do it, don't get scared, and abandon that ship," he yelled back to her, clapping in unsightly grotesque fashion. "Forget it, it's over; I'm out of this stingy lobster business! Watch me make even more profit on a reel taco shack, named Tacos de Pescado, bahaha!" Unable to muster the courage to swim past Slate, lucky to catch a ride on a local's jet ski.

Back on the ship, he blundered, "And where is my brother? Is he shopping again. I can't count on anyone!" Expenses are too high. Capt. Laiz is by his side with a new idea to be partners in a smoothie stand. Mrs. Waverly, adding banana chips to the menu because, "Why not." A hope that relied on an unnoticeable disguise, unlike her sister-n-law, she seemed oblivious to it all.

"I wouldn't mind staying," remarks Mrs. Waverly. "A fateful escape, we sure needed the break, just look at those waves."

"Glad we took a leap of faith," replied Mrs. Wits.

Business was swell, until reputation became their inevitable demise, not ending so well.

"What's going on ladies. Don't you see us in a bind?! Now, is not the time," said Capt. Wry-fi.

"Bro, watch how you speak to my lady mermaid," snarked Capt. Laiz, "I'm done with you being rude and untidy."

The disagreement did not last long on private property. Mama-Rouge protects egg bearing Roe from commotion of loose cannons. Twin-sister offers plenty of sea moss protein for sufficient energy; nourishing eggs is exhausting.

"Hey sis, maybe you'll have twin-tails like us, it's very likely!"

Not all swimmerets will survive the wide ocean. After carrying eggs, attached to her tail for nine months, few float to the surface; eventually, landing on the sea floor developing into heirs to the pier. Paparoa thanks Slate for an outstanding, stealthy response, "You're swift action protected our habitat."

A video that posted to social media raised reactions of admiration as crowds exited. Towns, cities and bureaus put signs outside businesses, "*Out of Lobster.*"

New laws banned seasonal lobstering, allowing a two-day max - mini season per year. Because, like the FWC officer believes... "All is fair in love and war," inevitably, raising the value. Crustaceans are protected, burrowing happily for next generations - having acquired skillful deft to do more, with having less.

Giacomo is popular at school, raising awareness for animals, which inspired him to volunteer at camp the following year. Seasons are changing, and still pregnant. Twice the size of her mate, slow-moving Roe, cautiously dwells in her haven, eggs in tote turning blue. Staying at the rock castle, avoiding sand-knolls for safe arrival of her little ones, choosing to birth at home.

"There's hope ahead, hang on!!" she shouts, "I may not be able to find all of you, but never, never forget, each of you are accounted for."

Tiny Lil 'roux grip tightly under her belly wherever she goes, reminding them, "None of you will ever be lobster bisque on my watch," she declared.

Largo requests his significant other to accompany him to a workout for claw rehabilitation. Instead, Roe cheered from the railing, careful not to overexert herself. Pals, Scuzzy and Scoozy, stop by to help carry the weight. Each week a mussel is added during crunches.

"Curl!" they tease... "one."

"That was ten crunches, c'mon stop," grunted Largo.

"Curl!" squids repeat "one" for each set, to trip his routine.

"This generation. Geez' how did I make it this far," he said, ultimately reaching his goal, "you're just too cool for school I guess."

Months of physical therapy, finally, accelerate re-growth of his main claw, slowly increasing strength.

"You will be in shape to hold your langostinos," said Scoozy.

"No, it's lobsterettes," disagree, fussy Scuzzy.

"Nooo, it's actually langostas!"

Largo puts an end to the dispute, "Way to blow this out of the water," he expressed walking away.

Largo spent winter bundled with Roe. Cooped up months, tempted to check the 'aqua net' out of boredom. "Love-bug, seen my sunglasses recently?" she asked, hubby-lobby.

"Ah, yea, we no longer live in fear, I gave them to Giacomo."

"That's great, a savvy break from technology! A wonderful way to assess the waters," she said.

He agrees, "Shore thing, who needs reels anyway."

One year later, as the final bell loom closer, Ms. Manners has one more small assignment, "Draw a picture of what you're excited for at sea camp this summer; and remember," she said, her voice gentle, "let creativity guide you."

The room was quiet as she admires their art. Taking shades from his backpack, Giacomo puts them on for insight. Checking the forecast, his face lit with glee. In fascination, he colors what he sees, a blue and red lobster on a reflective pier, cradling twin yellow Lil' roux swimmerets with blue limbs in a dried-up coconut shell. Unsure of the genders, until life's full cycle of maturity reveal. Largo, using the revival of both claws to hold them tenderly, as Roe chooses the names, Azul and Amarillo, even fewer and far between than predicted.

Two years later, salty-sweet personalities at almost two inches, twin double-trouble Azul and Amarillo, learned to scale back from danger. Regulations that saved three generations. Lil roux's still needs time to adhere to pier rules, learning to swim with the current.

Another school season. Student's drawings hang on the wall of Ms. Manners room from the previous years. It felt like yesterday burying Grandma-Lob.

Again, more waterfall of tears, spreading ashes in the water. An unbreakable bond the day OG-Lob passed away, not before telling twin tails to be quicker. The waters trust even thicker.

Magdeline sways a hose in her mouth, chanting, "Let waves barrel in remembrance!"

A glorious, dynamic, and powerful transcend back into the universe. Delphine formed a wave pool, "Hey guys, I've been in Key West mining gold, you should visit," she said to Roe, "a perfect distraction from gold diggers."

Octavia chimed in, "I hear there's a 'wall' even too risky for me to dive. Ha, that's fine, I'm safe right where I am."

"Well then, suit yourself, stay here, cause there is no help," replied Delphine.

Early that winter, Paparoa and Largo honored the family by starting a new tradition, to include everyone in cultivating a pearl farm. Oyster bedding begins by skillfully placing seeds, harvesting pearls, not yet to be seen. The anticipated dream, replicas of Roe's necklace-ring. Not eating oysters in months with 'R'; too harsh for the pair, teaching their children early, sometimes life's unfair. The phrase that made the twins rebel. Mama-Rouge disapproved, tucking her grand-lobbies in bed, she says, "You must think with your head... I love you to the moon."

Receiving news of Hurricane Irena with category 4 wind on the outskirts of land brings updates not many can comprehend. Azul and Amarillo climb over every rock, nook, and cranny, resembling a rollercoaster and spinning cyclones. Anything to avoid responsibilities, they hadn't a clue.

Family attribute it to creativity over instability.

"Look at you two go!" said the newly Grand-Rouge, "you move at the speed of lightening."

Amarillo and Azul amuse the hurricane party. When almost slipping, mother yelled, "Wait, I forgot, put on your inherited gold, a chain link to stay connected."

"Great idea, thanks Mama-Roe! Don't worry, we won't fall."

Each of their pinchers holding on tight, they continued the rollercoaster, shouting, "Wahoo, go faster!"

Running out of breathe, needing to hydrate, Papa-Largo says, "Slow down, save some water for the rest of us; you drink like a fish!"

After much loss and untimely destruction from devastation, the twins began to lack luster, behaving unbright.

"Stop, stop, stop... everything is fine," said new father, Largo. "Think of Grandpa-Lob when casting for fish, he would say, "Keep your eye on the prize, not to miss something divine," with fierceness in his eyes. He was a true gangster."

The motto kept true for Largo guarding his Lil' roux, not to be caught by surprise and sold for a bargain. It was time Azul and Amarillo are schooled, never shackled.

"Calm down, be wise, rationalize; and when in doubt, try to improvise," said Paparoa, from one shell to another.

Hence, the tail end.

Authors Bio

A passion for Fine Arts at an early age participating in theater. Love for theatrics continued over the years, when attending performing arts centers, musicals, and concerts. Traveling has been inspiration in life. Art never faded, working on many projects. Eventually, discovering a desire to write after receiving a 'literary vision,' inspiring to write a book about helping animals, people and the planet.

See Author's Page for upcoming book releases and dates.

www.ingramcontent.com/pod-product-compliance
Lightning Source LLC
La Vergne TN
LVHW040223110826
845146LV00004B/1270

* 9 7 9 8 9 9 2 5 1 9 9 1 4 *